MORTON AND SIDNEY

MORTON AND SIDNEY

Story and pictures by

CHRIS L. DEMAREST

Aladdin Books
Macmillan Publishing Company   New York
Maxwell Macmillan Canada   Toronto
Maxwell Macmillan International   New York   Oxford   Singapore   Sydney

For
J O H N

First Aladdin Books edition 1993. Copyright © 1987 Chris L. Demarest. All rights reserved. No part of this book may be reproduced or transmitted in any form or by any means, electronic or mechanical, including photocopying, recording, or by any information storage and retrieval system, without permission in writing from the Publisher. Aladdin Books, Macmillan Publishing Company, 866 Third Avenue, New York, NY 10022. Maxwell Macmillan Canada, Inc., 1200 Eglinton Avenue East, Suite 200, Don Mills, Ontario M3C 3N1. Macmillan Publishing Company is part of the Maxwell Communication Group of Companies. Printed in Japan.

10 9 8 7 6 5 4 3 2 1

The text of this book is set in 18 point American Typewriter Medium. The illustrations are rendered in watercolor and pen-and-ink.

Library of Congress Cataloging–in–Publication Data. Demarest, Chris L. Morton and Sidney / story and pictures by Chris L. Demarest.—1st Aladdin Books ed. p. cm. Summary: Morton helps his friend Sidney, a shy friendly monster, to regain his place in the closet where he lives. ISBN 0-689-71740-7 [1. Monsters—Fiction.] I. Title. PZ7.D3914Mo 1993 [E]—dc20 92-44153

Morton yawned. It was time to get up.

But something seemed strange.

Morton looked around his room.

"Sidney," cried Morton. "What are you doing
out of the closet? It's not nighttime."
"They kicked me out," said Sidney.

"They can't do that," said Morton.
"But they did," said Sidney.

"OPEN UP! OPEN UP! OPEN UP!"
shouted Morton. "Let Sidney back in!"

"NO, we won't," said Slimey Green.
"We don't want him here anymore."
"And you can't make us," the others chanted.

"Come on, Sidney," said Morton.
"I have an idea."

But his idea wasn't so hot.

Neither was his next one.

Sidney didn't seem to fit anywhere.

"This is no good," said Sidney. "And, besides,
    I don't want to live by myself."

Then Morton had another idea.
Quickly he and Sidney went to work.

When they were through, the biggest, ugliest, scariest monster in the world stood there.

Thwap. Thwap. Thwap. It headed for Morton's room.

"OPEN THE DOOR!" the big monster roared.

"Oh, my!" gasped Slimey Green.

"Gulp," went Big Oaf.

"How ugly," whispered Little Snout.

"Who are you? What do you want?"
they all asked.

"I've come to take Sidney's place,"
bellowed the big monster.

"Oh, no, you don't. We want Sidney!"
shouted the others. And away they flew,
looking for Sidney.

They searched the spooky basement.

They checked the attic

and every musty trunk.

They even looked in Morton's room.
Sidney was nowhere to be seen.

"Excuse me," said Morton. "I think I can help."

"Surprise!" called Sidney.
"Hooray!" cried the others.

That night everything was back to normal.